EPPING

ONCE UPON A TIMELESS TALE

The Emperor's New Clothes

STORY BY **HANS CHRISTIAN ANDERSEN**
RETOLD BY **MARGRETE LAMOND**

PICTURES BY
CAROL THOMPSON

LITTLE  HARE
www.littleharebooks.com

Once upon a time in a land far away—but not so far you couldn't get there in a day—there lived an emperor who was so pleased with his appearance that he stared at the mirror more than anything else in the world. His favourite thing to do was get dressed up, and then stare at himself some more. The higher his hat, the fluffier his frills, the happier he was. He changed his outfit before breakfast and after morning tea, halfway through luncheon and three times in the afternoon.

If people couldn't find him, all they had to do was look for his mirror, and there he would be, admiring himself.

Because the emperor's clothes were so fine, visitors came from all around to see the clothes for themselves. One day two gentlemen turned up in town. They were not especially honest, and they had devised a scheme to make a bit of money. The first thing they did was set up a shop. Outside the shop they hung a sign that said they were master weavers. Then they started to boast.

'Not only can we weave better cloth than anyone in the world,' they said, 'but our cloth is so fine, only special people can see it.'

Soon everyone in town knew about the master weavers. And everyone knew that only people who were clever, sensible and hardworking would see this magical cloth and the magical clothes the weavers made from it. Anyone who was lazy and stupid wouldn't see a thing.

When the emperor heard about it, he wanted some of these clothes for himself.

He imagined it would make his wardrobe more magnificent than ever. Better still, wearing magical clothes would be a crafty way of discovering which of his ministers were lazy and stupid. So he paid the master weavers several bags of money, supplied them with all the golden and silken thread they needed for weaving their cloth, and ordered them to weave and sew a full outfit for him in a month.

The master weavers set up their looms and got on with the job.

Their shuttles whizzed back and forth, the pedals clattered and the looms hummed and they made so much noise, and worked so long into the nights, that their neighbours couldn't sleep.

By the end of the first week, the emperor was so excited he only changed his outfit three times a day. By the end of the second week, he was only changing twice a day. By the end of the third week, he was so curious to know how the weavers were getting on, he almost went to lunch in his dressing gown.

But he was afraid of taking a look at the cloth for himself. What if he couldn't see it? Would everyone think he was lazy or stupid?

So the emperor sent his oldest, wisest and most trusted minister to have a look. The oldest minister would surely see the cloth—if ever anyone was wise and clever and hardworking, it was he—and he could come back and describe the cloth to the emperor.

The oldest minister went to visit the weavers.

There they sat in their shop, making a racket and working so hard the sweat ran into their eyes. But, to the oldest minister, the looms looked completely empty.

'Whatever will I tell the emperor?' he thought. 'If I say I can't see the cloth, he will think I am stupid and lazy. I must pretend I can see it.'

The weavers were as polite as anything. They leapt to their feet and bowed and smiled and pointed out the glowing colours and elegant patterns they had woven into the cloth.

Then they asked the oldest minister what he thought of the work so far.

'The cloth is magnificent!' he said. 'The emperor will be very pleased when he sees what you have made for him.'

The oldest minister went back to the emperor and told him that the cloth was the most magnificent he had ever seen. The emperor was relieved. Not only was the cloth magnificent, but his oldest minister had been able to see it, which meant he was clever, sensible and hardworking.

So, when the master weavers wanted more money, silk and gold, the emperor gave them even more than they asked for.

The final week went by. But the looms kept clattering day and night, and the cloth still wasn't finished. The emperor was so distracted and fretful that he went to dinner in his slippers. Even so he wasn't brave enough to look at the cloth for himself, just in case he couldn't see it. So he sent the next-oldest minister to see how it was coming along.

'Isn't this the most beautiful fabric?' the weavers said when the next-oldest minister arrived. 'Won't the emperor look wonderful when he wears his new clothes?'

The next-oldest minister, of course, could see nothing.

'Surely I am not stupid,' he thought to himself. 'And I work hard at my job. I will have to pretend I can see this fabric, or the emperor will kick me out.'

'It is truly superb,' he agreed.

And that's exactly what he told the emperor, too.

The emperor breathed a sigh of relief. If his oldest minister and next-oldest minister could both see the fabric, the time must surely have arrived when it was safe for him to see it for himself. The next morning he invited several guests to go with him, as well as the two ministers who had already seen the cloth, and they all crowded into the master-weavers' shop.

'Isn't this the most wonderful cloth you have ever seen?' said the oldest minister.

'Just look at how they have used the gold thread to make these intricate patterns,' said the next-oldest minister. 'Have you ever seen such an artistic arrangement of colours?'

'I can't see a thing,' thought the emperor to himself. 'I must take care not to let it show. I shall pretend I can see this cloth, or who knows what might happen!'

'Remarkable!' he cried aloud. 'Just as beautiful as everyone said. You must hurry and finish my outfit overnight.

Then we shall have a procession tomorrow to show off my new clothes. At the end of the procession I will award you with a Medal of Honour and pay you even more money.'

The weavers stayed up all through the night.

First they pretended to carefully snip the cloth from the loom. Then they pretended to cut and stitch a pair of breeches, a waistcoat, a shirt, a jacket, and finally a cloak with such a long train that six people would have to help carry it.

The next day they delivered the clothes to the emperor's chambers, and the first thing they did was shoo everyone else out of the room.

'These clothes are so fine and delicate,' they said, 'only we know how to handle them properly.'

They told the emperor to take off all his clothes. Then they pretended to help him into his new outfit.

'You see, your clothes are as light as a feather,' they said. 'You probably can't even tell you're wearing them!'

The emperor certainly couldn't tell he was wearing anything at all. When he looked in the mirror, he *still* couldn't tell. 'I do hope,' he thought to himself, 'that I am the only one who can't see these fabulous new clothes of mine.'

'How splendid you look!' the weavers cried. 'Every inch the emperor!'

'Truly splendid,' agreed the emperor.

When the emperor appeared at the door of his chamber, the lords and ladies were astonished to see him standing there with nothing on.

But they clapped and cheered, each trying to outdo the others.

'How splendid!' they cried. 'What glorious colours! What magnificence!'

The train bearers pretended to lift the train of the cloak from the floor and the emperor paraded back and forth.

Then the royal procession headed out into the street. Everyone knew about the magnificent magical clothes, and no one wanted anyone to think they were lazy or stupid, so everyone clapped and cheered as the emperor passed by.

'Truly fabulous!' they shouted as the emperor paraded down the street.

'Absolutely grand and marvellous!' they yelled as he paraded around the square.

'Totally and utterly splendid,' they roared as he paraded back to the palace.

'But he hasn't got anything on!' a little girl cried as the emperor paraded up the royal stairs.

'Hush!' whispered her mother. 'Don't let anyone know you can't see his clothes. They will think you are lazy and stupid and no good at your work.'

'But I am not lazy and stupid,' said the girl. 'And I have no work. And the emperor hasn't got any clothes on!'

The people standing next to the girl nodded their heads. 'It's true, you know,' they said. 'The emperor seems to be quite naked.'

More and more people began to murmur, and then to shout and point.

'The emperor is as naked as the day he was born,' the crowd eventually roared.

And so indeed he was.

The emperor's face turned bright red.

He felt sillier than a pumpkin on a peach tree, but he kept climbing the palace stairs until he was safe inside. Then he gave orders for every mirror in the land to be turned to face the wall.

And if things have not changed, that's how they still are.

～

As for the master weavers, some say they split their sides laughing. But whether they did or didn't, they were never seen again.

Which was just as well.

Little Hare Books
an imprint of
Hardie Grant Egmont
Ground Floor, Building 1, 658 Church Street
Richmond, Victoria 3121, Australia

www.littleharebooks.com

First published 2015

Cataloguing-in-Publication details are available from the
National Library of Australia

978-1-921894-99-2 (hbk.)

Designed by Vida & Luke Kelly
Produced by Pica Digital, Singapore
Printed in China by Wai Man Book Binding Ltd.

5 4 3 2 1

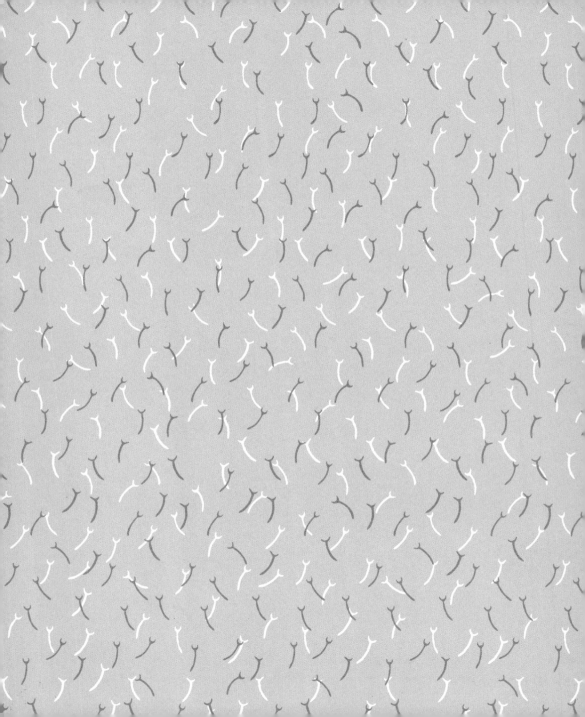